For my whole matzoh-ball-loving family.
I adore you.
And for my beloved, Rusty, I miss you madly.
B.G.

For my Airedale Terrier, Mack,
the most food-obsessed dog I've ever owned.
D.M.

From the publisher:
This book is a fantasy and in no way intends to give advice
about what to feed your dog. Please check with your vet
to make sure what is appropriate for your dog to eat!

Intergalactic Afikoman, 1037 NE 65th Street, #167, Seattle, WA 98115

www.IntergalacticAfikoman.com

Publisher's Cataloging-In-Publication Data

Names: Grubman, Bonnie, author. | Melmon, Deborah, illustrator.
Title: Bubbe and Bart's matzoh ball mayhem / Bonnie Grubman ; illustrated by Deborah Melmon.
Other Titles: Matzoh ball mayhem
Description: Seattle : Intergalactic Afikoman, [2021] | Interest age level: 003-008. |
Summary: "Bubbe and her puppy, Bart, are trying to get ready for Shabbat, when Bubbe's matzoh balls start flying"
--Provided by publisher.
Identifiers: ISBN 9781951365080 (hardcover)
Subjects: LCSH: Matzo balls--Juvenile fiction. | Dogs--Juvenile fiction. | Sabbath--Juvenile fiction. |
CYAC: Matzo balls--Fiction. | Dogs--Fiction. | Sabbath--Fiction.
Classification: LCC PZ7.G932 Bu 2021 | DDC [E]--dc23

Library of Congress Control Number: 2021938324

Printed in the USA
First Edition
2 4 6 8 10 9 7 5 3 1

FSC
www.fsc.org
MIX
Paper from
responsible sources
FSC® C008080

BUBBE AND BART'S
MATZOH BALL MAYHEM

Bonnie Grubman

Illustrated by

Deborah Melmon

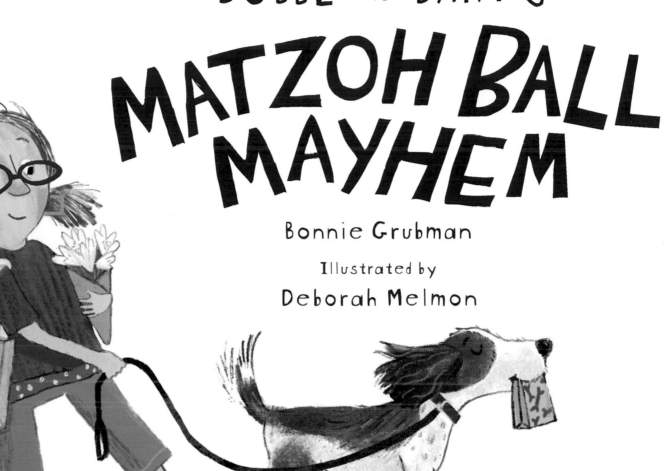

INTERGALACTIC
Afikoman

SEATTLE

This is Bubbe's story.
Believe me that it's true.
Her puppy loved each Friday night
like Jewish puppies do.

When Bubbe made her matzoh balls,
Bart was at her feet,
waiting for a ball to fall,
and not some doggie treat.

"No begging, Bart,"

said Bubbe, and pointed to the floor.

She offered him a liver stick.
But Bart just begged some more.

Then, OY GEVALT, what happened next would cause you minor shock.
While Bubbe manned the matzoh balls, she heard a weird

K-KNOCK

THUMPITY went the matzoh balls,
and foam began to rise.

The broth began to gurgle, and the balls increased in size.

So Bubbe turned the knob to low, just to keep them warm.
But her broth would not stop foaming, and bubbled up a storm.

Then the pot began to rattle, CLINKITY . . . CLANKITY,

BOOM!

Bubbe watched ONE matzoh ball zoom across the room.

Bubbe stared in disbelief,
too stunned to make a kvetch.
And her jaw dropped even lower,
when Bart sped off to fetch.

Now the pot began to wobble, and Bubbe felt her heart.
Then **TWO** more matzoh balls

PA-CHOOOONGED...

and so did hungry Bart.

So Bubbe found a better lid, and some very sticky tape.
She sealed it like a package, so nothing would escape.

But OY! That tape ripped open,
such tsuris, unexpected.
And Bart wolfed down a triple treat
when **THREE** more balls ejected.

Then Bubbe heard a rumble,
which caused her soup to splash.
FOUR more balls poured down like rain
and vanished in a flash.

Now things began to stir again, but Bubbe yelled, "DON'T FEAR!"
So Bart, though full and out of steam, grabbed his baseball gear.

Bubbles gushed and overflowed, yet Bubbe kept her wits.
When **FIVE** more balls flew overhead, they caught them
in their mitts.

Now **SIX** more balls erupted,

and these magicians acted quick.

Bubbe and her buddy Bart

staged their clever trick.

Bubbe and the Great Bartini

Finally, the kitchen hushed, and the matzoh balls stayed still. Bart curled up in his cozy spot beneath the windowsill.

Now simmering in the soup pot were SEVEN balls
(you guessed!) floating, oh so peacefully,
like the seventh day of rest.

Bart helped set the table
in gleaming pearly white.
And they welcomed Bubbe's family
on this special Friday night.

Then Bubbe lit the candles,
and blessed her precious Bart.
She sang the kiddush with her pup,
and tore the challah apart.

The gefilte was devoured.

The soup was dynamite.

The matzoh balls were nothing less
than magic and delight.

The babka was delicious.
The key lime was sublime.

"Shabbat Shalom, sweet Bubbe.
We had a lovely time."

Now Bubbe took her shoes off,
and enjoyed a calm Shabbat.
Happy no more matzoh balls
were escaping from her pot.

YUP! This is Bubbe's story,
and Bart's own tall tail too.
(WOOF) Jewish pups love Friday night . . .

and zany mayhem too.

GETTING READY FOR SHABBAT

Shabbat is a very special day of the week... a day for rest and relaxation, a day for spending time with family and friends. We wish one another, "Shabbat Shalom," which literally means "Sabbath Peace." Traditionally, Shabbat is greeted with the blessing over the Shabbat candles and sanctifying the day with the blessing over the wine and challah. Then we eat a special Shabbat meal (which might just include matzoh balls).

But before we can celebrate Shabbat, we must get ready. Getting ready for Shabbat can be as simple as cleaning up our house, putting some flowers on our table or dressing up in special Shabbat clothes. Or it could be as elaborate as making homemade challah, gefilte fish or matzoh balls. Sometimes the minutes before Shabbat starts can be a bit zany, as we busily finish our last-minute preparations.

But then comes Shabbat . . . and Shalom.

GLOSSARY

BABKA — a Jewish dessert, often with chocolate or cinnamon
BUBBE — grandmother
CHALLAH — braided egg bread for Friday night
GEFILTE FISH — an Eastern European Jewish preparation for fish, often served as balls or loaves
KIDDUSH — the blessing over the wine
KVETCH — a complaint

OY GEVALT — Yiddish exclamation of amazement and distress
SHABBAT SHALOM — a Sabbath greeting, wishing a peaceful Shabbat
TSURIS — trouble

For Bubbe's Magical Matzoh Balls and a super-fun Shabbat treat for your Jewish dog, please visit www.IntergalacticAfikoman.com

As a child growing up in New York City, it wasn't unusual to find little BONNIE GRUBMAN on her fire escape with a stack of books, immersed in fiction and mesmerized by the brilliant illustrations. Nowadays, the veteran early childhood educator is dedicated to preserving the magic of childhood by creating her own stories that will make children wonder, laugh out loud and open their minds to all possibilities. Bonnie and her husband live in the suburbs. They have two grown children, exhilarating twin grandsons, and fond memories of their distinguished rescue dog, Rusty... who was a clever food thief with skilled paws, and a pure heart.

Encouraged by her high school art teacher, DEBORAH MELMON began her professional career painting storefront windows during the holiday seasons. After graduating from Academy of Art University in San Francisco, her artwork launched the advertising campaign for Legoland in San Diego and she created murals for two discovery rooms at the California Science Center in Los Angeles. She has illustrated over fifty children's books for clients that include Viking Children's Books, Scholastic, Parragon UK, Boyds Mills & Kane, Kar-Ben Publishing, Penguin Young Readers Group, and Sleeping Bear Press. Deborah lives in the San Francisco Bay Area. Learn more at deborahmelmon.com and on Instagram @deborahmelmon.

BART